PROFESSOR I.Q. EXPLORES THE SENSES

by Seymour Simon

illustrated by Dennis Kendrick

PROFESSOR I.Q. EXPLORES THE SENSES

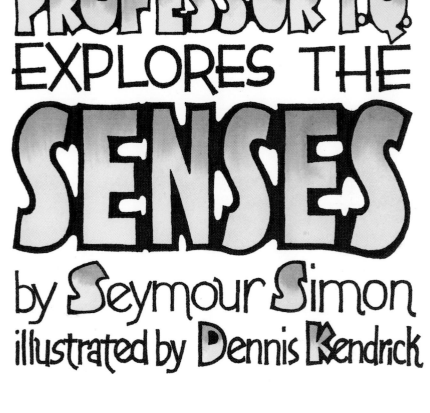

by Seymour Simon

illustrated by Dennis Kendrick

BELL BOOKS

BOYDS MILLS PRESS

Published by Bell Books
Boyds Mills Press, Inc.
A Highlights Company
910 Church Street
Honesdale, Pennsylvania 18431
Printed in Hong Kong

Publisher Cataloging-in-Publication Data
Simon, Seymour.
    Professor I.Q. explores the senses / by Seymour Simon ; illustrated by Dennis Kendrick.
[48]p. : col. ill. ; cm.
Summary: Easy-to-understand text for the beginning reader.
ISBN 1-878093-28-2
1. Senses and sensation—Juvenile literature. [1. Senses and sensation.]
I. Kendrick, Dennis, ill. II. Title.
612.8—dc20   1993
Library of Congress Catalog Card Number: 91-77615

First edition, 1993
Some of the material in this book appeared in a different form under the title *Finding Out With Your Senses* published by McGraw-Hill, 1971.
Book designed by Kathleen Westray
The text of this book is set in 14-point Optima and Palatino.
The illustrations are done in pen and ink and watercolors.
Distributed by St. Martin's Press

10 9 8 7 6 5 4 3 2 1

For Michael and Debra—long life
—S.S.

To Andy with love
—D.K.

Every day is a good day to explore the world around you.

Look at a high-flying kite and changing cloud shapes in the sky.

Listen to your friends at play and the sound of the rain.

Stroke a cat's smooth fur and a rough tree trunk.

Smell what someone is cooking for dinner.

Eat a pickle and chew a stick of peppermint gum.

You can find out about so many things
by seeing,
        hearing,
                touching,
                      smelling,
                            tasting—
by using all your senses.

Each day there's something different for you to see and to hear.
Each day brings something else to touch, to taste, and to smell.
Where can you find new things to explore with your senses?
They are in your room, in the kitchen, in your classroom, out-of-doors, everywhere!

TOUCHING

TASTING

SMELLING

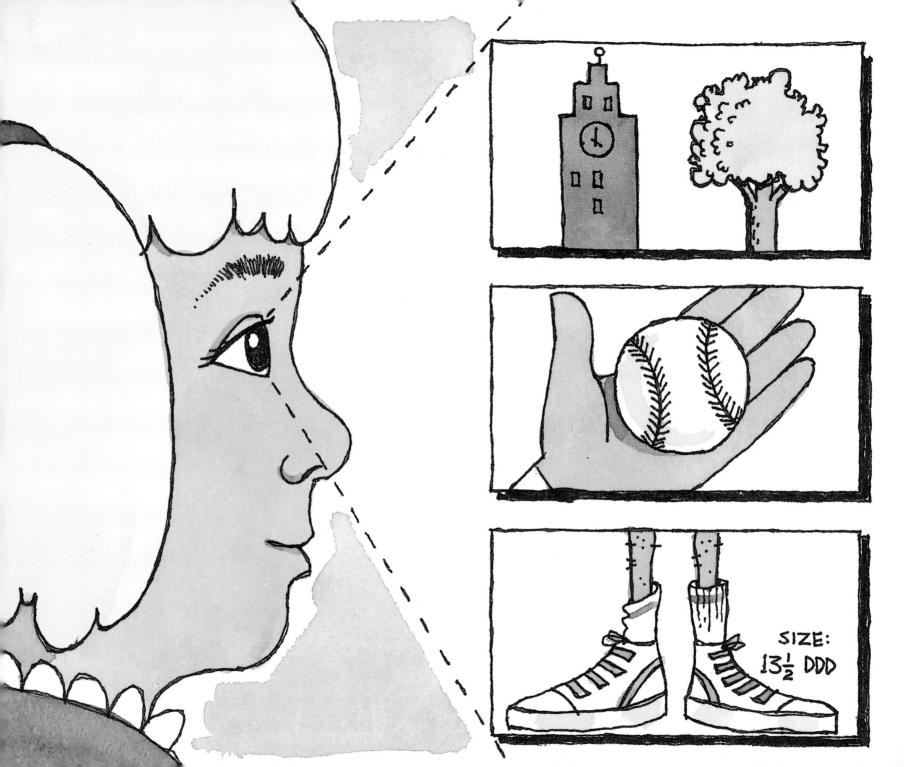

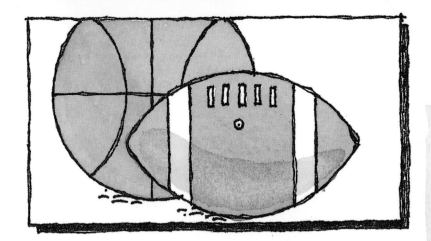

Seeing is one way of finding out with your senses.
You can often tell the size of some things by looking at them.
Is the building taller than the tree?
Is the ball the size of your hand?
Which of your friends wears the biggest sneakers?

You can also tell the shape of things by looking at them.
Does a basketball have the same shape as a football?
Do all tree leaves have the same shape?
Can you tell the difference between a milk container and a soda bottle by their shapes?

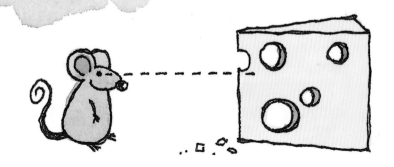

Sometimes it's not easy to tell the size or shape of an object. From the ground, a high-flying airplane looks very tiny. From the airplane, people walking on the streets below look as small as ants. How big does the moon look to you? Look at close-up photos of the moon taken by astronauts. You can see that the moon is really very big. But the farther away an object is from you, the smaller it looks. You are far away from the moon. That's why it looks so small. From where you are on Earth, you can block out the entire moon with just your thumb. Try it out.

THE **EYES** HAVE IT !!!

Stars look like bright spots in the night sky.
The stars are really as big and bright as the sun.
But the stars are so far away that they look tiny.
Many stars are so far away that you can't see them
at all unless you look for them with a telescope.

Look at a grain of sand and the head of an ant. Can you tell what is their shape or which is larger? Some things are too small for you to see them clearly. Other things are so small that you can't see them at all unless you look through a magnifying lens or a microscope.

Try to catch a soft rubber ball thrown high in the air.
Now close one eye and try to catch it again. Watch out!
It's much harder to catch a ball using only one eye.

Close one eye again.

Try to bring your two index fingers together tip to tip.

Now try it with both eyes open.

Using two eyes helps you to see how near or far things are.

What else can you see by looking?
Look at a green leaf, a red fire engine, the blue sky.
You can see many different colors around you.

What colors can you see in a room,
in a picture book,
on your clothing,
out in the street?

Mix paints of different colors to see what new colors you can make.

Mix some blue and some yellow paint to make green.

Paint some of the green color on paper to keep a record.

Add a little more blue or a little more yellow.

Paint the new color on the same piece of paper and compare the two.

Keep on adding a little bit of blue or a little bit of yellow.

Record each new color on the paper.

How many colors can you make?

Mix other colors together.

Mix red and blue to get purple.

Mix yellow and red to get orange.

Try your own mixtures and see what you get.

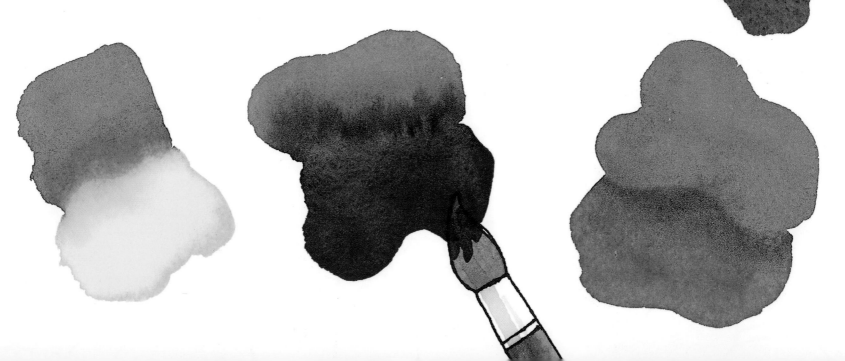

Sunlight looks white but it really is made of many different colors.
You can see the colors that make up white light when you see a rainbow.
The colors are called the spectrum. They are always arranged in the same
order: red, orange, yellow, green, blue, and violet.
The edge of a mirror or a glass prism in sunlight shining on a white paper shows
a spectrum.

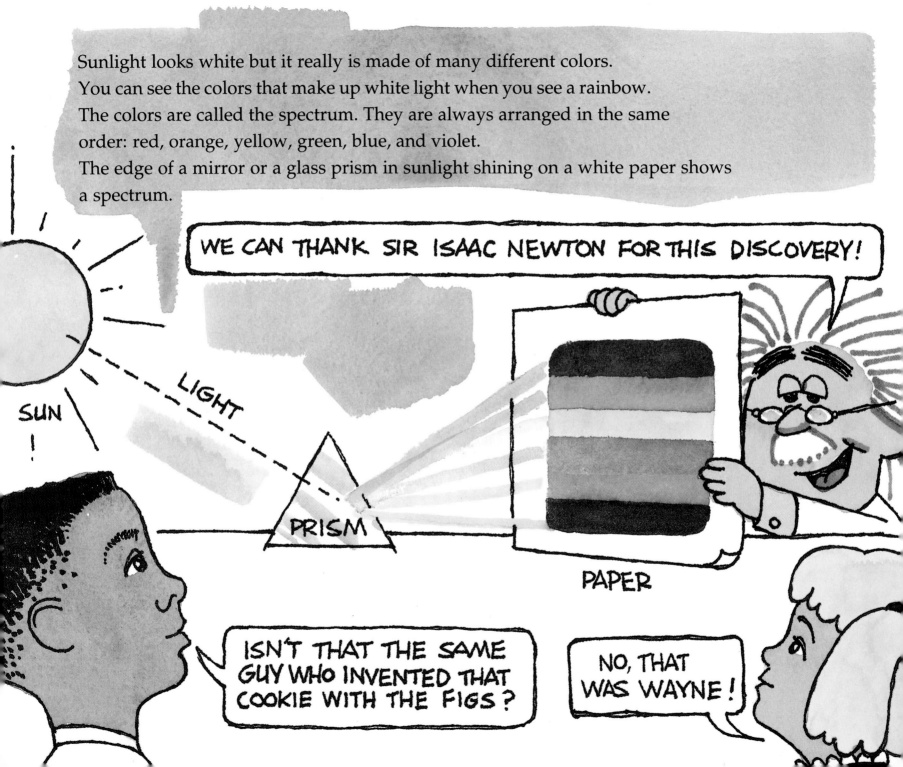

Find some colored bottles or a piece of colored plastic to look through.
Imagine that you are a visitor from outer space and can only see
through red or green or blue.
Look at the world around you through a piece of red, green, or blue plastic.
Do things look the same?

Look at things that are moving and things that are still.
Look at shiny things and dull things.
Look at things you can see through and things you can't.
You can find out a lot about things by looking at them.

You can find out other things about objects even when you cannot see them. Close your eyes and listen. There are sounds all around you. Can you tell the difference between the sounds you hear? Listen to the sounds of cars and trucks passing by on your street. Listen to the songs of birds and the barking of a dog. Listen to the voices of your friends at play and the sounds of their footsteps.

TICK
TOCK
TICK
TOCK

You have to listen more carefully for some other sounds.
Listen to the wind in the trees
or the rain falling against your window.
Listen to the soft boom of a distant thunderclap
or the quiet ticktock of an old pocket watch.

You can make all kinds of other sounds.
Walk on dried leaves and listen to them crackle.
Snap your fingers, clap your hands, whistle and sing, laugh and cry.

You can make things that make sounds.
Shake some pebbles in a small milk carton
to make a rattle.
Lightly tap a tall thin drinking glass
with a pencil.
Add a little water to the glass and tap
it again.
How does the sound change?
Use different-sized glasses with different
amounts of water and tap them to make
other sounds.

Blow across the top of a soda bottle.

Blow hard, blow soft.

Blow across the tops of different bottles.

What gives a high note?

What gives a low note?

What gives a loud sound?

What gives a quiet sound?

Try arranging different bottles in a row to play a tune.

Make a plucker by stretching a rubber band between two nails on a board.

Twang the rubber band with your finger.

Stretch the rubber band on nails farther apart and twang it again.

Try stretching nylon fishing line, string, wire, and thread.

How are the twangs different?

You can find out about lots of things by listening carefully.

How can you tell the difference between different cloths
that are the same color?
Touch a piece of wool, a piece of cotton, and a piece of silk or nylon.
One feels rough, another feels smooth, and still another feels slippery.
Can you tell which is which?

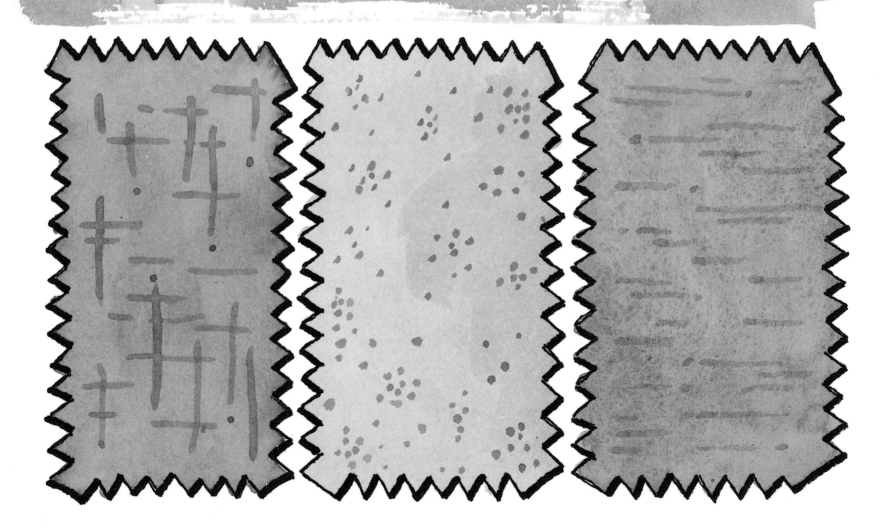

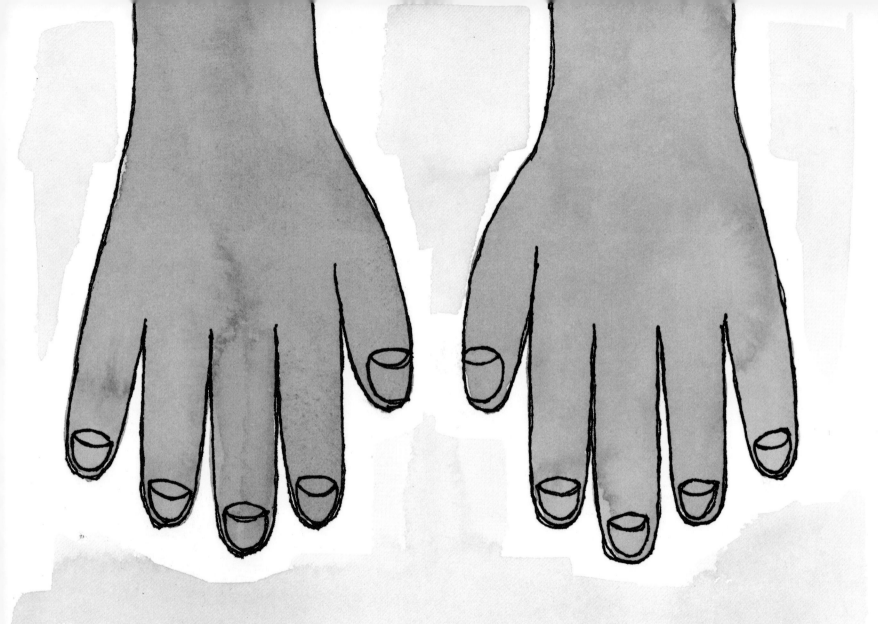

You can use any part of your body to touch things, but you usually use your fingers to find out how things feel.

Put all kinds of things in a shoe box:
marbles, cotton balls, rocks, pencils, a block of wood, rubber bands,
paper clips, sandpaper, a moist sponge, a metal spoon, and so on.
Close your eyes and put your hand in the box.
Just by touching, try to tell what each object is.

Let a friend try.
Ask her to close her eyes or wear a blindfold.
Then let her take an object from the box and
tell how it feels.
She may say that an object feels
            rough or smooth,
                light or heavy,
                    round or long,
                        flat or thick.
She may also say that an object feels
cold or warm, or even wet or dry.
Your sense of touch tells you many things.
Try it out.

You taste with your tongue and smell with your nose.
Some tastes are easy to tell.
Taste a piece of sugar.
Rinse out your mouth and taste a slice of lemon.
Rinse again and taste a salty peanut.
Rinse again and taste a drop of black coffee.
Sweet, sour, salty, and bitter are easy tastes to tell.

Other tastes are harder to tell.

Taste a piece of bread, a raisin, a carrot, a tomato, milk, and fruit juice.

Many foods have more than one taste.

They may be sweet and salty or any other mixture.

Some odors are pleasant to smell.

You may like to smell flowers, or perfume, or a favorite food.

Other odors are not very nice:

a car's exhaust, rotting food, or burning rubber.

Some odors are easy to tell:
ammonia, vinegar, or an angry skunk.
Other odors are more difficult to describe:
the seashore, the pages of a new book, chalk dust on a blackboard,
your wool jacket when you come in out of the rain.

Taste and smell are sometimes mixed up with each other.
When you say that a piece of apple pie is delicious,
you probably mean that it both tastes and smells good.

Try this with a friend.
Blindfold him with a handkerchief.
Tell him that you are going to give
him certain foods to taste and that
he is to try to tell you what they are.
After he is blindfolded, give him
a slice of apple to taste and, at
the same time, hold a piece of onion
under his nose. He probably will
say that he is eating an onion.
Now ask your friend to hold his nose
and give him a slice of onion to taste.
He may have a hard time telling what
it is without being able to smell it.
When you have a cold and have
difficulty breathing through your
nose, you may think that the food
you eat has lost its taste.
That's because it's often difficult
to tell the taste of foods without
also smelling them.

You see your friends smile at you and hear them laugh.

You stroke a friendly dog and rub a pet rabbit's fur.

You smell the spring rain and the newly mowed grass.

You enjoy the taste of food.

You are always using your senses when you explore the world.

Seymour Simon has written more than one hundred highly acclaimed science books for young readers, many of which have been selected by the National Science Teachers Association as Outstanding Science Trade Books for Children. He lives in Great Neck, New York.

Dennis Kendrick has illustrated many books for children, a number of them in collaboration with Seymour Simon. His titles include THE SANDLOT, MONSTER BIRTHDAY, and STORIES ABOUT ROSIE. He lives in New York City.